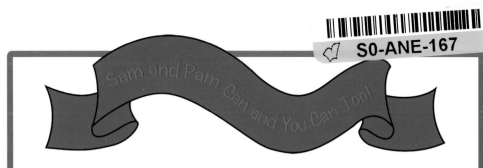

Sam and Pam Can and You Can Too!

We Can Ride Our Bikes

by Amanda Litz

illustrated by
Cynthia Garcia

Traveler's Trunk Publishing
Cedar Springs, Michigan

To Jacob, Sierra, Mason, and Ethan –
you can do anything you put your mind to.
– A.L.

ISBN 978-0-9841496-2-9

CPSIA facility code: BP 313627

www.travelerstrunkpublishing.com

Printed in the United States of America

I am Sam.

I am Pam.

We are twins.

But we are
not the same.

I like to eat apples.

I like to eat carrots.

I know how to
play football.

I know how to
play checkers.

We have two bikes,
one for each of us.

We can ride our bikes.

First we have to be safe.

I have a helmet
for my head.

I can put the helmet
on my head.

I have pads
for my elbows.

I can put the pads
on my elbows.

I have pads
for my knees.

I can put the pads
on my knees.

We are ready to
ride our bikes.

Mom pushes me on my bike.

I can pedal with my feet.

Dad pushes me on my bike.

I can go fast on my bike.

Mom and Dad let
go of our bikes.

Look, we can do it
on our own.

Now it is time to
put our bikes away.

Mom and Dad said
we did a good job.

We like to ride our bikes.

Can you ride a bike?

What can you do?

Sam and Pam
are proud of
you!